The Usborne Little Children's Travel Activity Book

James Maclaine

Designed and illustrated by

Erica Harrison, Benedetta Giaufret,
Enrica Rusinà, Laurent Kling, Mattia Cerato,
Lauren Ellis and Agostino Traini

Additional designs by Alice Reese

Edited by Fiona Watt

You'll find the answers to the puzzles
on pages 61-64.

On the road

Find the stickers for these pages in the middle of the book. Then, stick each one on top of the label it matches.

yellow taxi

green car

blue bus

vrroomm

red truck

moo

orange motorbike

pink car

white van

zoom

quack

quack

blue car

red bicycle

beep

red car

purple car

3

Departures

There's lots to spot at this airport.
Can you find...

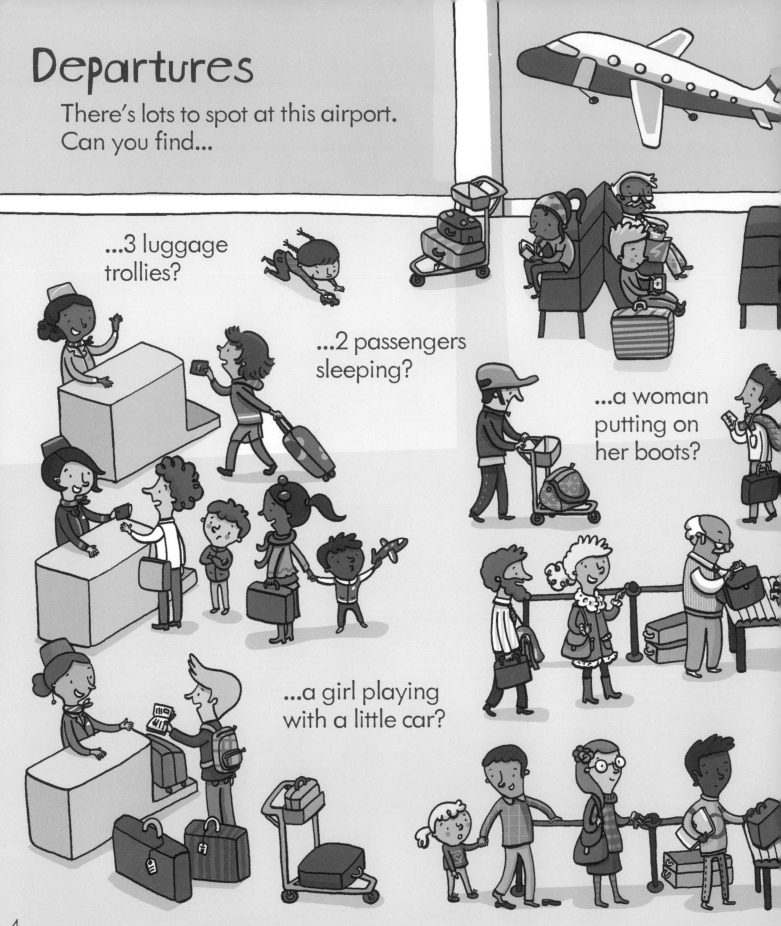

...3 luggage trollies?

...2 passengers sleeping?

...a woman putting on her boots?

...a girl playing with a little car?

...3 stripy suitcases?

...a boy playing with a toy plane?

...a girl taking photos?

5

Take the train

Complete the picture with a black pen.

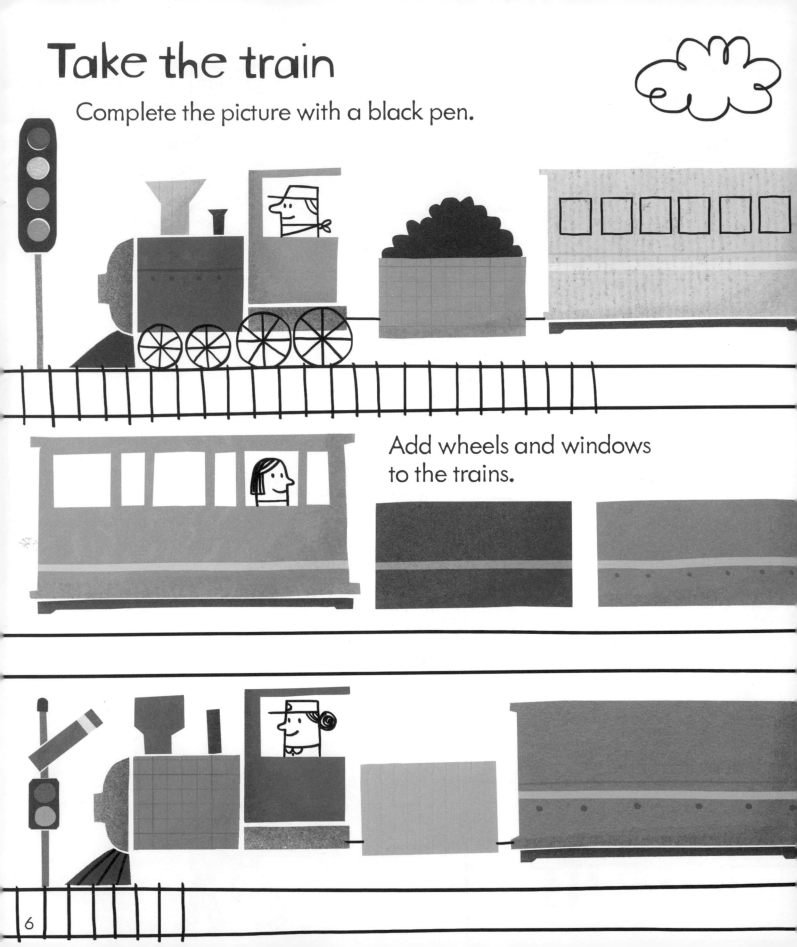

Add wheels and windows to the trains.

Doodle birds and passengers, too.

Finish drawing the train tracks.

7

On the beach

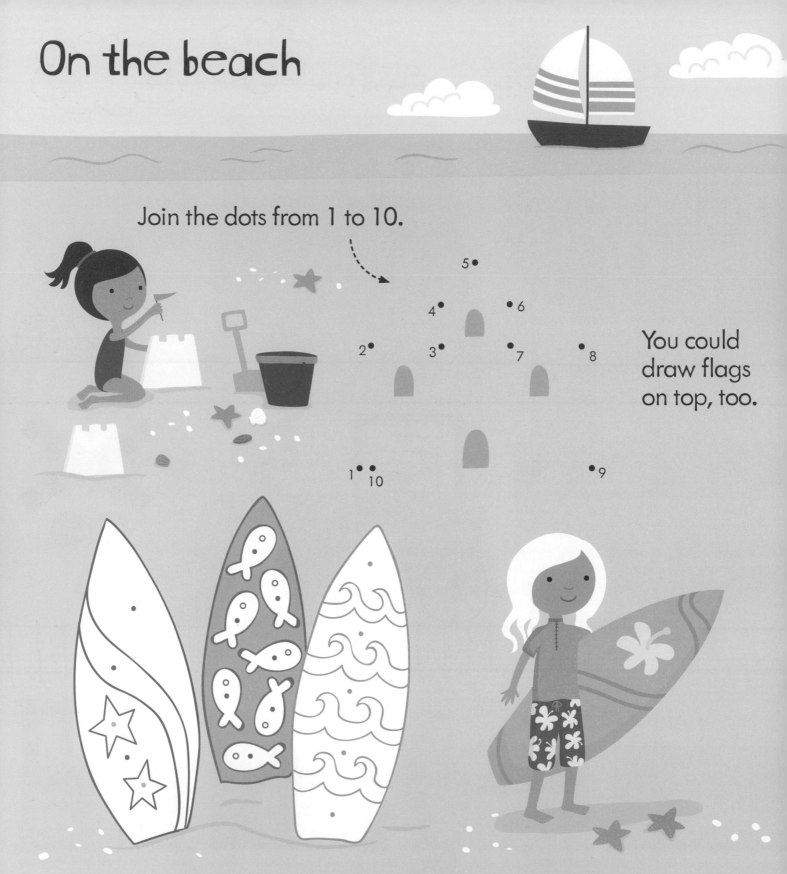

Join the dots from 1 to 10.

5
4   6
2   3   7   8

You could draw flags on top, too.

1 10   9

Colour the surfboards with pens that match the spots.

Draw over the dotted lines to finish the kites.

Which seagull is the odd one out? Draw a ring around it.

Snowy slopes

Count how many people are skiing and how many are snowboarding.

There are .... people skiing and .... people snowboarding.

How many animals can you spot enjoying the snow, too? ....

Draw a line leading the sledge down the slope, passing around each of the flags from 1 to 10.

Give each snowman a face, some buttons and a hat.

Pitching camp

Find the red tent sticker on the sticker pages. Then, stick it on the map so it's...

• east of the lake
• west of the sheep
• and north of the trees.

Put the pictures in the order they happened.
Number them from 1 to 4.

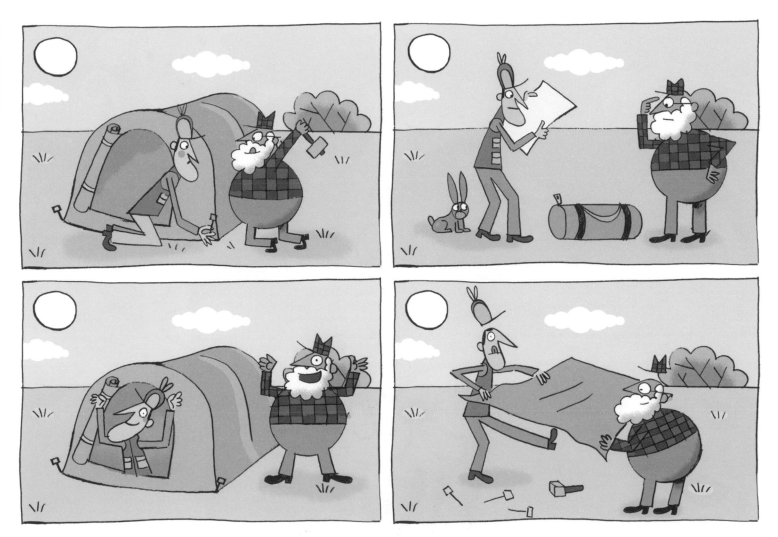

Which camper van is different? Draw a circle around it.

Jungle life

Colour in the animals
on these pages.

Draw more black
stripes on the tiger.

Add more spots to the leopards.

15

At the market

The children are thinking about what they want to buy. Draw lines from the children to the stalls they need to go to.

Flora's Flowers

Holiday Hats

Baked today

Draw over the dotted lines in blue to finish the fountain.

How many pigeons
can you spot?   ....

Ice cream

Souvenirs

Summer Style

Fresh fruit

Making a splash

Draw a line as quickly as you can down the slide. Try not to bump into the sides with your pen.

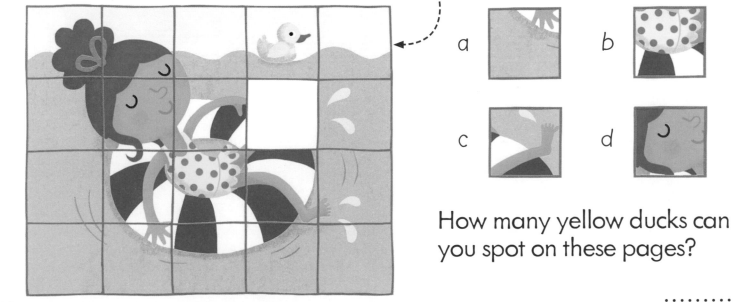

Which square completes this picture puzzle? ....

a

b

c

d

How many yellow ducks can you spot on these pages?

....

Colour in the swimmers' costumes to match their swimming caps.

Draw goggles on some of them, too.

Town travel

Read the bus route, then lead the bus around the town past all the places in the right order. Draw a line to show the way it goes.

Bus route

Bus station
Museum
Hospital
Zoo
Market
Cinema
Football stadium
Airport

Zoo

Cinema

Usborne FC

Up in the air

Can you find and colour...

...2 spotty hot-air balloons?

...a jumbo jet?

whirrr

22

...2 stripy planes?

whoosh

...a plane with 2 pilots?

...3 helicopters?

whizzz

...3 birds that aren't flying?

At sea

Draw a line between each pair of boats.

Which boat is the odd one out?

John
Dory

Finn

Who has caught the most fish?

. . . .

Ray

Can you spot
the crab?

25

Packing up

Can you help the children pack?
Find the missing items on the sticker
pages and stick them in the suitcases.

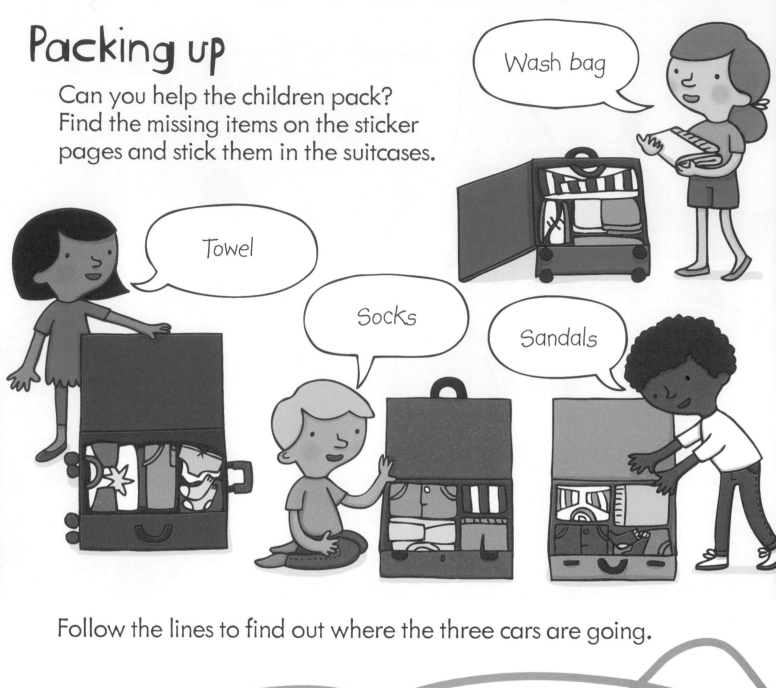

Follow the lines to find out where the three cars are going.

Read Harry's list and look at the picture. What is missing?
Draw a line under the word.

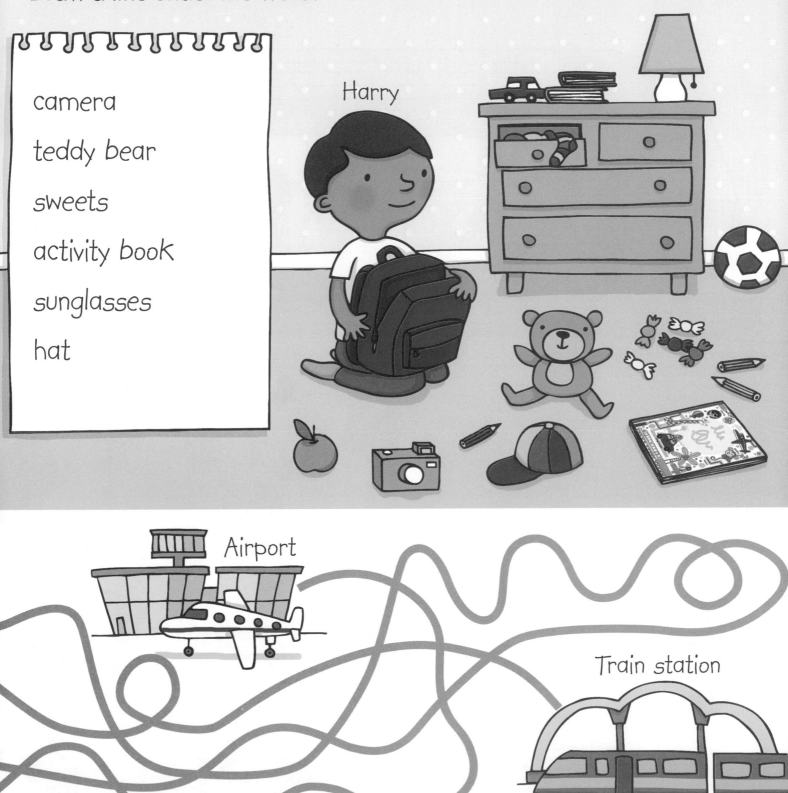

camera

teddy bear

sweets

activity book

sunglasses

hat

Harry

Airport

Train station

Platform puzzles

Oh no! Simon has lost his ticket. Draw a circle around the ticket when you spot it.

Simon

Can you find Jack?

- Jack is on the train.
- He is wearing a T-shirt.
- He has curly hair.
- He likes to read.

Hi Jenny

Hi Alex

Which girl is Jenny and which is Alex? Follow each speech bubble to find out.

Picture postcards

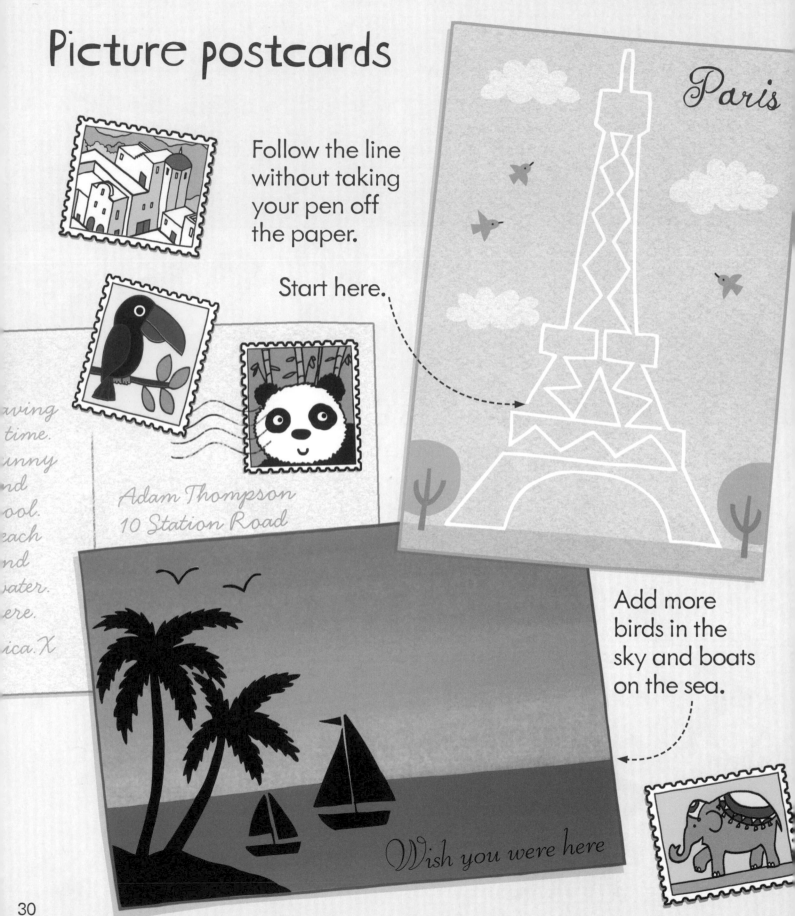

Follow the line without taking your pen off the paper.

Start here.

Paris

Adam Thompson
10 Station Road

Add more birds in the sky and boats on the sea.

Wish you were here

Fill in the shapes with pens that match the spots.

LONDON

Join the dots from 1 to 9.

Draw rings around the five differences between these two pictures.

Beachwear

Press on the stickers from the sticker pages to get these children ready for the beach.

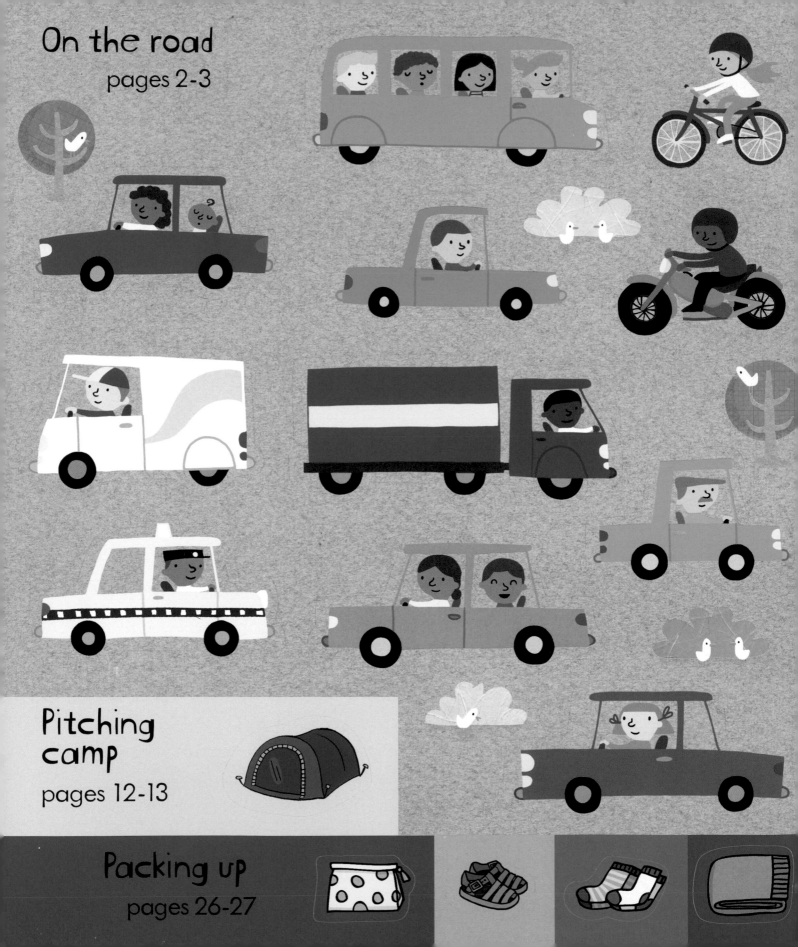

On the road

Pitching camp

Packing up

Beachwear   page 32

Harbour view   pages 38-39

Time to eat
pages 46-47

Space travel   pages 52-53

H

p

Under the sea

Doodle a face on each of the underwater creatures including the shells.

Pedal power

Can you spot...

...a dog?

...a tricycle?

...a black helmet?

...a bike with 2 people on it?

...a bike with a very big wheel?

Draw lines to join the cyclists with their matching helmets and bikes.

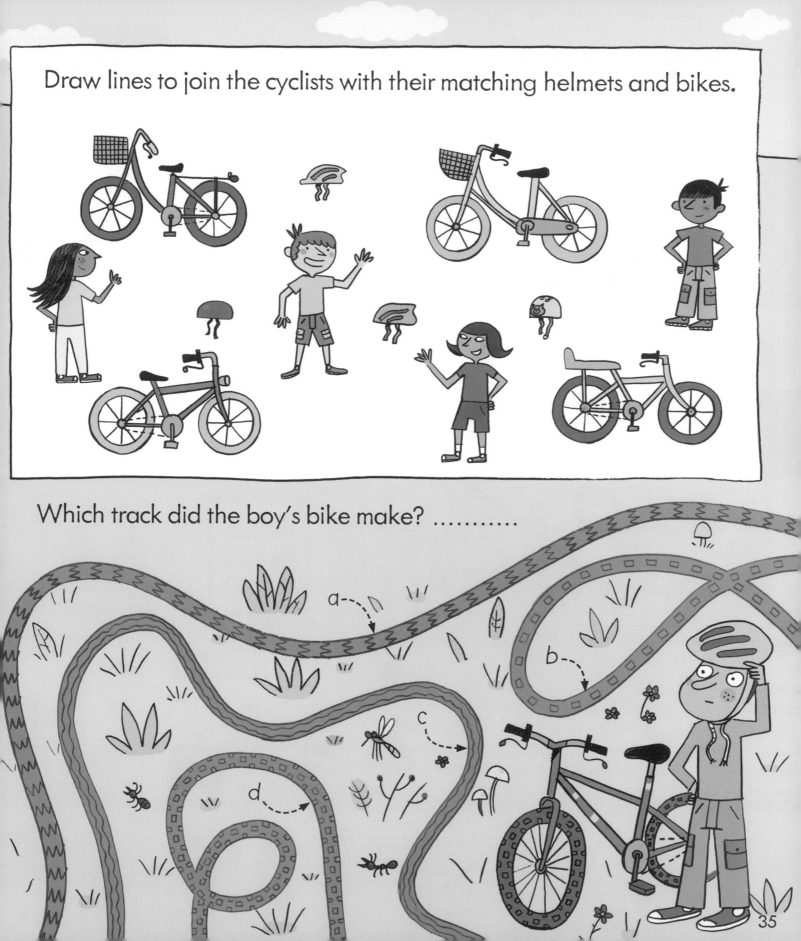

Which track did the boy's bike make? ....

To the platform

Draw a line leading this man from the car park to the train.

36

How many clocks can
you find in the picture? ....

Draw a circle around each one you spot.

Harbour view

Match the building stickers to the shapes here and stick them down.

Can you guide this little tug through the maze of boats to the big red ship?

Look out for a yellow submarine, too.

Airport arrivals

Can you spot five differences? Draw around each one.

Whose passport photos are these?
Find the people in the queue.

Can you help the passengers find their luggage?
Draw lines to show each one the way.

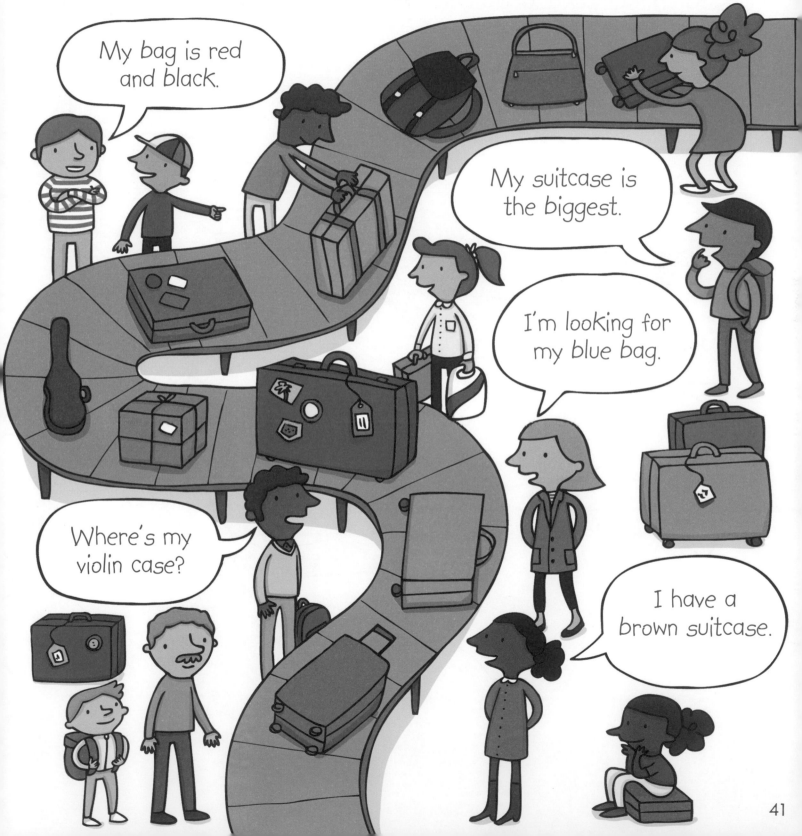

Rockpool hunt

Search the rockpool and the shore.
Write the number of each thing
you see below the pictures on the
opposite page.

I can see...

4

On the move

Draw a line leading the plane through the clouds as quickly as you can.

Count how many red cars and how many blue cars are in the two long rows.

☐ red cars ☐ blue cars

Draw hot-air balloons in the sky by following these instructions.

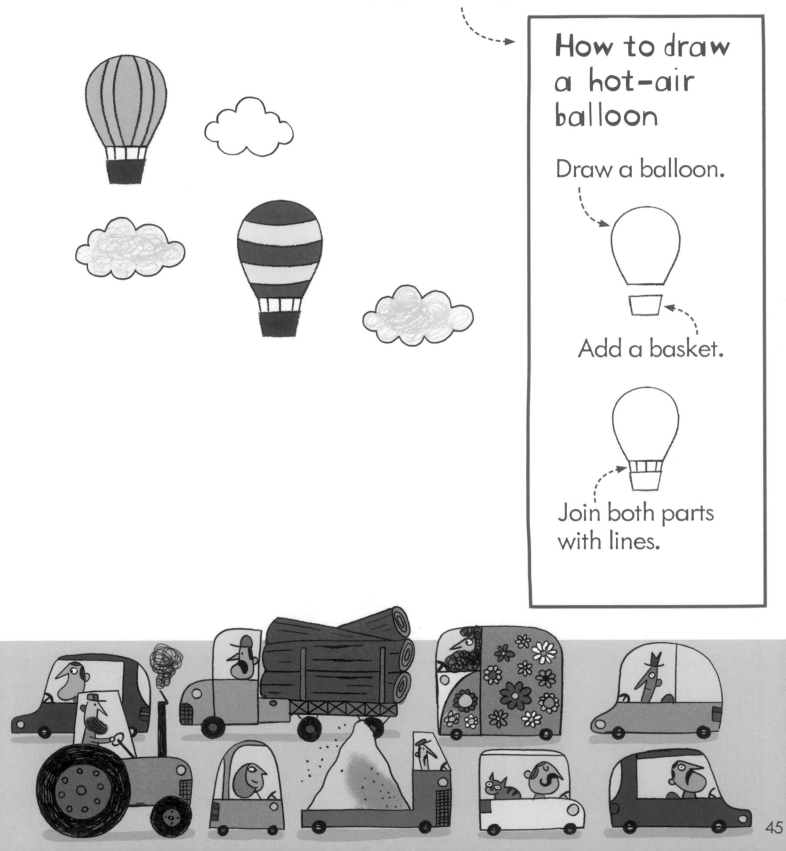

How to draw a hot-air balloon

Draw a balloon.

Add a basket.

Join both parts with lines.

Time to eat

Complete the meal. Draw...

...meatballs and spaghetti...

...fizzy bubbles...

...and watermelon pips.

Put these pictures in the correct order. Number them from 1 to 3.

What's missing from the barbecue in picture b?

Add the stickers of ice creams to give the children the flavours they want.

Strawberry

Mint choc chip

Vanilla

Chocolate

Where in the world?

New York

Los Angeles

Brasília

Santiago

Can you work out where Anna is on the map?

She's in the square where there are...

- trees
- mountains
- and a lake.

Write her name in the square.

Moscow

Berlin

Rome

Cairo

Beijing

New Delhi

Nairobi

Cape Town

Sydney

Draw a line showing the plane's route from Sydney to Brasília. It must stop at Beijing, Nairobi, Rome and New York, in this order, on its way.

On safari

Sophie

Which photo has Sophie just taken? ....

a

b

c

Which zebra is the odd one out?

Draw a curly mane around this lion's head.

Put the giraffes in height order. Label the shortest one 1 and the tallest one 5.

Space travel

Complete the picture with the space stickers from the sticker pages.

Build a rocket

Stick on a rocket body.

Add a nose cone...

...and flames at the end.

Add star and
planet stickers
in the sky, too.

Fill the planet with aliens. Stick different
bodies and heads together.

Holiday hotel

Can you spot ten differences between this picture...

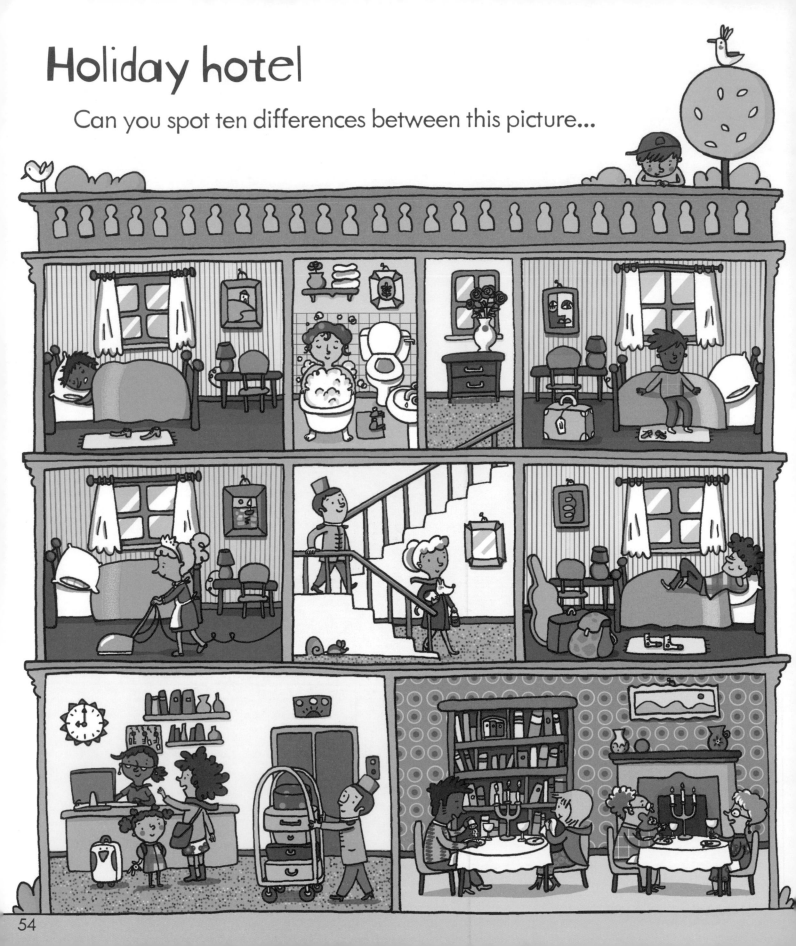

...and this one? Draw a ring around each difference.

Travel fun

Fill in the shapes. Each number stands for a different colour.

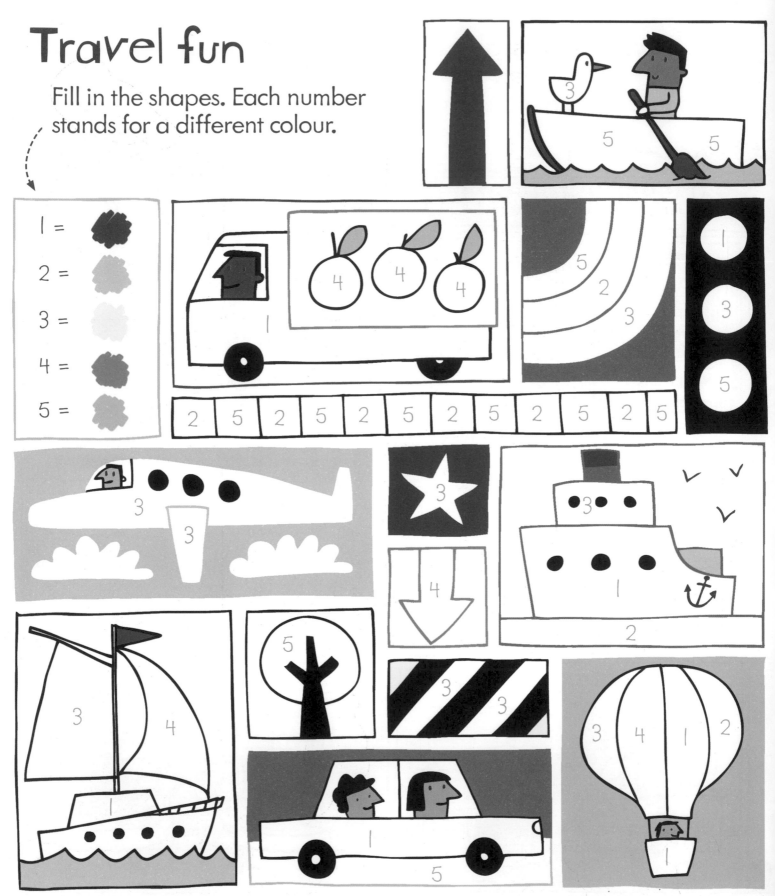

1 =
2 =
3 =
4 =
5 =

Find the passenger stickers on the sticker pages. Then, stick each one on top of the window it matches.

Usborne Activity Books

Route 123

Add the pigeon stickers, too.

Park life

Can you spot two identical birds in the tree?

How to draw a duck

Draw a circle for its head.

Add a body and a wing.

Then, give it a beak and an eye.

Draw more ducks on the pond and colour them in.

Which girl is Lily? Look at the picture and read the clues, then draw around her.

- Lily is sitting down.
- She has long hair.
- She is wearing sunglasses.

Can you find Hugh, too?

- Hugh has dark hair.
- He isn't wearing shoes.
- He is playing with a toy.

Holiday snaps

Fill this holiday photo album with the stickers from the sticker pages. Match each one to its label.

Rock climbing

On the beach

Ice cream

Swimming

At the zoo

My new friends

Answers

4-5 Departures

- ⭘ luggage trollies
- ⭘ sleeping passengers
- ⭘ woman putting on her boots
- ⭘ girl playing with car
- ⭘ stripy suitcases
- ⭘ boy playing with plane
- ⭘ girl taking photos

8-9 On the beach

This seagull only has one leg.

10-11 Snowy slopes

There are 7 people skiing and 4 people snowboarding.

There are 7 animals to spot.

12-13 Pitching camp

Stick the red tent here.

This van's wipers are pointing in a different direction.

16-17 At the market

There are 10 pigeons in the picture.

18-19 Making a splash

Square c is missing from the puzzle.
There are 6 yellow ducks.

20-21 Town travel

22-23 Up in the air

- ○ spotty hot-air balloons
- ○ jumbo jet
- ○ stripy planes
- ○ plane with 2 pilots
- ○ helicopters
- ○ birds that aren't flying

24-25 At sea

Finn has caught the most fish.

crab

26-27 Packing up

Harry's sunglasses are missing.

The red car is going to the train station.
The green car is going to the airport.
The blue car is going to the bus station.

28-29 Platform puzzles

---- This is Jack.

- ○ Simon's ticket

I'm Alex.

I'm Jenny.

30-31 Picture postcards

34–35 Pedal power

- ○ dog
- ○ tricycle
- ○ black helmet
- ○ bike with 2 people on it
- ○ bike with a very big wheel

The boy's bike made track d.

36–37 To the platform

○ There are 6 clocks.

38–39 Harbour view

○ submarine

40–41 Airport arrivals

42–43 Rockpool hunt

- ○ 4 🐟
- ○ 5 🦀
- ○ 7 🌸
- ○ 3 🐚
- ○ 6 🥅
- ○ 7 🪣
- ○ 1 🦐
- ○ 6 🕊

44-45 On the move

There are 5 red cars and 4 blue cars in the rows.

46-47 Time to eat

48-49 Where in the world?

Anna is in this square.

50-51 On safari

Sophie took photo c.

This zebra is missing a stripe.

You should number the giraffes from left to right: 4, 2, 3, 1, 5

54-55 Holiday hotel

58-59 Park life

These birds are identical.

I'm Hugh.

I'm Lily.

First published in 2013 by Usborne Publishing Ltd., Usborne House, 83-85 Saffron Hill, London EC1N 8RT, England. www.usborne.com © 2013 Usborne Publishing Ltd. The name Usborne and the devices ⚬⚬ are Trade Marks of Usborne Publishing Ltd. All rights reserved. No part of this publication may be reproduced, stored in a retrieval system or transmitted in any form or by any means, electronic, mechanical, photocopying, recording or otherwise without the prior permission of the publisher. UKE. Printed in Spain.